JANUARY

S	M	T	W	T	F	S
		1	2	3	4	5
6	7	8	9	10	11	12
13	14	15	16	17	18	19
20	21	22	23	24	25	26
27	28	29	30	31		

FEBRUARY

S	M	T	W	T	F	S
					1	2
3	4	5	6	7	8	9
10	11	12	13	14	15	16
17	18	19	20	21	22	23
24	25	26	27	28		

MARCH

S	M	T	W	T	F	S
					1	2
3	4	5	6	7	8	9
10	11	12	13	14	15	16
17	18	19	20	21	22	23
24	25	26	27	28	29	30
31						

APRIL

S	M	T	W	T	F	S
	1	2	3	4	5	6
7	8	9	10	11	12	13
14	15	16	17	18	19	20
21	22	23	24	25	26	27
28	29	30				

MAY

S	M	T	W	T	F	S
			1	2	3	4
5	6	7	8	9	10	11
12	13	14	15	16	17	18
19	20	21	22	23	24	25
26	27	28	29	30	31	

JUNE

S	M	T	W	T	F	S
						1
2	3	4	5	6	7	8
9	10	11	12	13	14	15
16	17	18	19	20	21	22
23	24	25	26	27	28	29
30						

JULY

S	M	T	W	T	F	S
	1	2	3	4	5	6
7	8	9	10	11	12	13
14	15	16	17	18	19	20
21	22	23	24	25	26	27
28	29	30	31			

AUGUST

S	M	T	W	T	F	S
				1	2	3
4	5	6	7	8	9	10
11	12	13	14	15	16	17
18	19	20	21	22	23	24
25	26	27	28	29	30	31

SEPTEMBER

S	M	T	W	T	F	S
1	2	3	4	5	6	7
8	9	10	11	12	13	14
15	16	17	18	19	20	21
22	23	24	25	26	27	28
29	30					

OCTOBER

S	M	T	W	T	F	S
		1	2	3	4	5
6	7	8	9	10	11	12
13	14	15	16	17	18	19
20	21	22	23	24	25	26
27	28	29	30	31		

NOVEMBER

S	M	T	W	T	F	S
					1	2
3	4	5	6	7	8	9
10	11	12	13	14	15	16
17	18	19	20	21	22	23
24	25	26	27	28	29	30

DECEMBER

S	M	T	W	T	F	S
1	2	3	4	5	6	7
8	9	10	11	12	13	14
	17	18	19	20	21	
29	30	31				

Glue

This book is dedicated to the founding mothers and fathers of
Read to Grow (providing books for babies and to the children in our community):
Roxanne Coady, Donna Lechner-Gruskay, Janet Weiswasser, Karen Pritzker-Vlock,
Annie Garcia Kaplan, Jennifer Aniskovich, Jane Ash, Robin Baker, Brian Condon,
Laurie Friedler, Ellen Frieler, Wendy Gifford, Susan Katz, Candy Kohn, Nancy Kyger, Roberta Lockhart,
Lisa Maass, Gini and Jack Mariotti, Virginia Mathews, Roslyn Meyer, Christine Mace, Ann Nyberg,
Laura Radulski, Susan Richman, Priscilla Russo, César Rodriguez, Laurel Shader, Kim Spencer,
Katie and Jonathon Stein, Sheila Wartel, Mary Lee Weber, and Carol Weitzman

To quote Margaret Mead—"Never doubt for one moment that a group of thoughtful,
committed citizens can change the world; indeed, it's the only thing that ever has."

—N.E.W.

Recycle Every Day!

Written and Illustrated by
Nancy Elizabeth Wallace

Marshall Cavendish
New York

Outside it was raining. Inside Minna was sitting on a chair singing,

"Recycle. Recycle. Recycle."

"Why are you singing 'recycle,' Minna?" asked Mom.

"The children at school have been asked to make posters about recycling. The ones that get picked will be in the Community Recycling Calendar. I'm trying to think of a really different idea for my poster."

"What does 'recycle' mean?" asked Pip. "Is it like a bicycle?"

Minna giggled. "Recycling is when you reuse or fix things instead of throwing them away."

"Did you know we recycle all the time?" asked Dad. "We can help you with ideas."

On **Monday**, they looked through their closets and dressers.

"I haven't worn this in years," said Mom.

"I really grew," said Minna.

"This never fit," said Dad.

"Look, Minna, I grew too," said Pip.

They bundled up the clothes and brought them to . . .

"Passing along clothes in good condition to others is a form of recycling," said Mom.
"That would make a terrific poster."

"I'm still thinking," said Minna.

On **Tuesday**, Minna and Dad cleaned up the yard.

They put all the leaves and grass and weeds into . . .

the compost maker.

"This will turn into nice rich soil for our garden," said Dad.
"And what a super idea for your poster!"

"I'm still thinking," said Minna.

On **Wednesday**, Minna, Pip, and Mom gathered up all of their empty cans.

They brought them to . . .

the return machines at the recycling center.

SCRUNCH, thoing. SCRUNCH, thoing.

"What's happening inside that machine, Minna?" Pip asked.

"The machine is squishing the cans. Then they will be made into new cans," she explained.

RECYCLE CANS

Put cans in here

push

coin return

Little Tote

Pip danced. "Look, Minna, I'm doing the cancan. The can machine is a good idea for your poster, Minna."

"I'm still thinking," said Minna.

On **Thursday**, Minna and Mom got their tote bags.

the grocery store.

In the cereal aisle, Minna pointed. "There's the recycling symbol. These boxes were made from recycled paper. That means trees were saved!"

"That's why we use tote bags, too, " said Mom. "Is our trip to the grocery store giving you any ideas for your poster, Minna?"

"I'm still thinking," she answered.

On **Friday**, Minna and Pip looked through their books. "When I was a tiny baby, I liked this one," said Pip.

"*The Magic Carrot Patch!*" said Minna. "That used to be my favorite. I must have read it a million times."

Minna and Pip piled up seven books.

They took them to . . .

Books for Every Bunny.

"Thank you," said Mrs. Libro. "We'll give your gently used books to children who might not have any. Every bunny needs a book!"

"Look, Minna, posters!" said Pip. "Are you still thinking?"
Minna nodded.

On **Saturday**, they had supper.

When they finished, Minna helped . . .

wrap the leftovers.

"To reduce waste, use plastic containers instead of plastic wrap," said Dad. "Will that idea work for your poster?"

"I'm almost done thinking," said Minna.

On **Sunday**, Mom asked, "Isn't the art for the poster contest due tomorrow?"

Minna nodded. She began to sing,

"Recycle on Monday.

Recycle on Tuesday.

Recycle on Wednesday."

Suddenly Minna knew what she wanted to do.

Minna gathered scissors, a glue stick, markers, and her pink polka-dot pencil. She got out her box of used envelopes, old folders, and scraps of found paper.

Then she started to work.

The next day, Minna brought her poster to school.

"Please, please, please pick mine," she whispered to herself.

Monday, **Tuesday**, **Wednesday**, and **Thursday** went by. Finally it was the day when the children would find out whose posters had been chosen for the calendar.

Mr. Turner, the First Selectman, spoke at the school assembly. "If everybody does their part, together we can make the world a cleaner, greener place!"

March, Carrie.

Reuse Plastic Bottles
Carrie

April, Lexi.

GIVE TOYS

you don't play with anymore
to others
Lexi

May, Tyrone.

BUY BIG
A BIG CONTAINER=

LESS DUMPING IN THE DUMP
Tyrone

September, Lauren.

October, Dave.

November, Miguel.

And for December . . . "

Minna whispered to herself, "Please, please, please ."

"Vanessa!" said Mr. Turner. "Vanessa's poster shows us how to make a bird feeder by recycling a plastic milk container. What a wonderful December holiday gift it would make."

An old milk container

is for the birds

by Vanessa

"This will be our best Community Recycling Calendar ever!"
said Mr. Turner. "I want to close today with . . .

our cover artist, Minna! She even used recycled paper. Minna's poster tells us to '*Re-re-re*member, *re-re-re*cycle every day.' Say it with me."

"*Re-re-re*member, *re-re-re*cycle every day.'"

"Everybody!"

"RE-RE-REMEMBER, RE-RE-RECYCLE EVERY DAY!"

Recycle Game

Be the player with the most "tiny trash" in your recycling bin. (2-4 players)

Materials for Each Player:

A clean **8-ounce plastic container** with a lid. (A recycled margarine container with a lid works well.)

A **coin**.

"Tiny trash" made from recycled materials. (For example: **21** small squares cut from a cardboard food box, a clean Styrofoam™ food tray, or a milk carton; **21** small balls of aluminum foil; **21** packing peanuts; **21** bottle caps)

To play:

Open the book to the game board and lay it flat.

Choose a group of "tiny trash" and an empty plastic container.

1. To start the game, put one piece of your "tiny trash" on the blue sunrise square.

2. The first player tosses the coin. Heads means move 1 space, tails means move 2. When your playing piece lands on **red**, put an object from your pile on Earth in the center of the game board. By doing this, **you are dumping** things on our Earth that could be recycled. When your playing piece lands on green, put a piece of "tiny trash" from your pile in your plastic container (your "recycling bin"). By doing this, you are recycling.

3. When a player lands on the black night space, the players should count the "tiny trash" in their "recycling bins." Whichever player has the most "tiny trash" did the most recycling for that game day!

When you are finished playing, put the "tiny trash" in the plastic containers and put the lids on. Keep the containers and the coin in a recycled zipper bag for the next time you play.

Really Recycle Activity

(A recycling challenge for you, your family, and your class at school.)

1. Find containers and make or gather piles of "tiny trash" from recycled objects.
   (You can reuse what you made for the recycling game.)

2. Find a large, empty, clear plastic container with a wide mouth and a lid.

3. Each time you *really* reduce, reuse, or recycle materials, put a piece of "tiny trash" in the container. For example, if you use a paper bag to wrap a gift, put one of your "tiny trash" pieces in the large, clear container. (If you have trouble thinking of ideas, look through the pages of *Recycle Every Day!*)

4. At the end of the day, the "tiny trash" in the large, clear container shows how much recycling you and others did. Dump out the "tiny trash." Count it. Ask each person to tell what he or she recycled during the day. If you like, you can keep a daily chart and record your progress.

Make recycling a habit, every day!
When we all work together, you can see how much can be done to take care of our Earth!

Author's Note

Writing a book about recycling has been exciting! My husband Peter and I try very hard to do the **three R's** of recycling:

Reduce—fixing things instead of throwing them away.

Reuse—using things again and again; giving things that we don't need anymore that are in good condition to others.

Recycle—putting newspapers, cans, cardboard, aluminum foil, bottles, and plastic containers in the recycling bin every week so they can be made into newspaper, metal, cardboard, aluminum, glass, and plastic products.

Since writing and illustrating *Recycle Every Day!*, I have been trying to do even more to *re*duce, *re*use, and *re*cycle. What if everybody did? We could change the world we live in!

Your friend,

Nancy Elizabeth Wallace

Nancy Elizabeth Wallace

Can you find these recycled papers and materials in the illustrations?

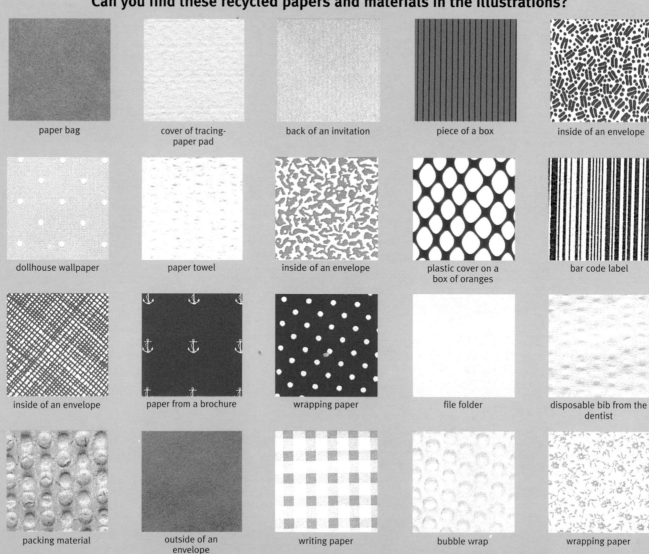

paper bag	cover of tracing-paper pad	back of an invitation	piece of a box	inside of an envelope
dollhouse wallpaper	paper towel	inside of an envelope	plastic cover on a box of oranges	bar code label
inside of an envelope	paper from a brochure	wrapping paper	file folder	disposable bib from the dentist
packing material	outside of an envelope	writing paper	bubble wrap	wrapping paper

Library of Congress Cataloging-in-publication Data
Wallace, Nancy Elizabeth.
Recycle every day! / written and illustrated by Nancy Elizabeth Wallace.—1st ed.
p. cm.
Summary: When Minna has a school assignment to make a poster about recycling, her entire rabbit family spends
the week practicing various kinds of recycling and suggesting ideas for her poster.
ISBN: 0-7614-5149-8
[1. Recycling (Waste)—Fiction. 2. Refuse and refuse disposal—Fiction. 3. Rabbits—Fiction.
4. Animals—Infancy—Fiction. 5. Schools—Fiction.] I. Title.

PZ7.W15875 Re 2002
[E]—dc21
2001026050

Creative Director: Bretton Clark

Designer: Victoria Stehl
Editor: Margery Cuyler

The illustrations in this book were prepared with cut paper, markers, and colored pencils.

Printed in Malaysia
First edition

4 6 8 10 9 7 5 3

www.marshallcavendish.us